# IVOR
## the engine
# Snowdrifts

Story by OLIVER POSTGATE

Pictures by PETER FIRMIN

Snow was falling in the top left-hand corner of Wales. Flakes the size of old pennies floated gently from the dark grey sky and laid themselves carefully on the ground.

There was so much of it!

The little town of Llaniog, high in the
hills, was quite covered.
The roads were blocked.
The railway was blocked.
People dug paths from door to door but
the snow soon covered them again.

Ivor the Engine was snug and warm in his
shed on the siding. So were the sheep who
had come down off the hill to warm themselves by his boiler. In fact, there were
sheep everywhere in the town. They huddled
in the High Street and clustered around
Eli the Baker's shop, where the smell of new-
baked bread floated out among the snowflakes.

Eli the Baker was a very worried man.
The storeroom where he kept his flour was
usually full to the ceiling with flour bags,
but now it was empty. He had used up all
the flour. He put on his overcoat and scarf
and tramped out into the snow.

On the way he met Mr Davies the Grocer
and Mrs Williams the Sweetshop.

"What are you out of then?" asked Eli.

"Everything," replied Mr Davies. "Rice,
treacle, butter, jam, biscuits, potatoes.
You name it, I haven't got it. My shop is
almost empty!"

"So is mine," sighed Mrs Williams.

Dai Station the Station-master and Jones
the Steam the engine driver, sat in the
booking office at Llaniog Station with
their feet up on the stove, drinking tea.

There came a knock at the door. It opened and in came a lot of cold air, some snowflakes, Eli the Baker, Mr Davies and Mrs Williams.

"What's this?" asked Dai Station. "There are no tickets or trains today."

"No flour," said Eli.

"No potatoes," said Mr Davies.

"No bull's-eyes," said Mrs Williams.

"Oh yes," said Dai Station, "what are
you going to do about that then?"

"There's nothing we can do," growled Eli.
"The flour is waiting at Grumbly Town for
Ivor to collect as usual. Until it comes
we shan't have any more bread."

"Or potatoes," said Mr Davies.

"Or jelly-babies," said Mrs Williams.

"Oh, there's tragedy now," said Jones.
"What shall we eat?"

"We shan't eat, we shall starve," explained
Eli the Baker, "unless you and Ivor go to
Grumbly and collect the goods."

"But the snow is deep on the line,"
said Jones the Steam. "We would never get
through without a snowplough!"

"Then get a snowplough," said Eli the Baker firmly and went home.

Well, of course, Eli the Baker was quite right. The only thing to do was to get a snow-plough.

Jones the Steam and Dai Station took their feet off the stove, finished their tea and went to see Beynon the Smith.

"Snowploughs is it?" said Beynon Smith
thoughtfully. "I've no idea what snowploughs
look like, so I suppose I shall just have
to invent one. It would be a sort of double
sideways shovel, I expect. Something like
this perhaps . . ."

Beynon Smith took a piece of burnt
wood from the forge and drew on the wall.

"A bolt here at the back, look, and a bracket over Ivor's buffers of two-inch angle, riveted plates . . ."

Once Beynon Smith is busy inventing something, there is no point in standing about. He was still drawing and talking to himself as Jones and Dai walked back to the station. Jones the Steam went on

down to the shed to see to Ivor's fire and
tell him about the snowplough.

Beynon Smith did not waste time. He
hammered and thumped and welded sheet and
angles and bars of steel in his forge, and
by midday he was to be seen dragging a
strange implement over the snow like a
sledge.

He bolted it on to Ivor's front end,
over the buffers. It fitted very well.

"Go on, Ivor!" said Beynon. "Take a run
at the snow!"

Jones the Steam opened Ivor's regulator
as wide as it would go and Ivor fairly
charged at the deep snow. The snowplough
dug its point in and threw the snow up each
side of the line in a great shower.

"Keep going, Ivor!" shouted Beynon Smith as he jumped on to the step.

Ivor kept going and carved a clean path through the snow up to Llaniog Station.

There they coupled up two trucks and were ready to go to Grumbly.

"Shall we try it then, Ivor?" asked Jones.

POOP-POOP! went Ivor's whistle.

CHUFF CHUFF CHUFF went Ivor's pistons.
SCRUNCH . . . ER . . . SLURP . . . went
the snow as it was hoisted up and thrown
aside by the snowplough.

"Keep pushing, Ivor!" shouted Beynon Smith
and Dai Station as they disappeared down
the line.

The snowdrifts lay thick on the sides of
the hills but Ivor charged into them and
split them like meringues.

"Keep pushing, Ivor!" shouted Jones the
Steam, but Ivor needed no encouragement.
His fire was burning well, his steam pressure
was high. His pistons were puffing powerfully
and the snow was leaping up and away on
each side of them. He was enjoying himself.

It was a glorious sight. Even the sun
came out to see and lit the mountains with
shafts of light that glittered on the snow and
ice like golden fire.

Soon they came to Grumbly Town.

Jones closed the regulator and they rolled quietly into the snow-covered station.

"Are you there Mr Thomas?" shouted Jones the Steam.

Mr Thomas, the Station-master, took his feet off the stove and put down his mug of tea.

"What's this, the Ghost Train?" he laughed. "I didn't expect to see you again till after the snow!"

"Well, it's a bit of an emergency, like," explained Jones. "Eli the Baker is out of flour, Mr Davies has no potatoes and Mrs Williams is dangerously low on bull's-eyes. We can't let the town starve, can we?"

"Well, it's all waiting here for you,"
said Mr Thomas. "I'll help you load up."
There were fifteen bags of flour, five
of potatoes, nets of carrots, sprouts, onions
and leeks. Boxes of bull's-eyes and beef-cubes,
camphor, combs and caraway seeds, detergents
and dolly-mixture, embrocation, flannel
nighties, grapefruit, hatpins, hair oil,
honey and so on right through the alphabet.

Also there was Miss Figgin's old uncle, who had come to see the dentist three weeks ago, and had had to stay ever since.

They wrapped him in blankets and packed him in with the rest of the goods.

"Mind how you go now, Ivor," said Mr Thomas. "That's a heavy load you are pulling, look, and don't bump Mr Figgin too much or he'll have to come back for a new lot of teeth!"

POOP-POOP
CHUFF CHUFF CHUFF CHUFF.
The load was very heavy but as they had
cleared the line on the way down, Ivor
pulled it with no trouble. They puffed
merrily up the hill, through Tan-y-Gwlch
and down the hill beyond the tunnel.

Then they saw trouble ahead.

Where the line went close under the hill
the snow had slipped in an avalanche, and
the line was blocked.

"Take a run at it, Ivor!" shouted Jones,
"We've plenty of weight behind us!"

Jones opened the regulator.

POOP went Ivor's whistle as he charged
joyfully at the snowpile.

SCREECH-SLITHER ... BONK-BONK ... CLUNK.

Ivor had slammed on his brakes.

He stopped inches from the snowpile.

"What's wrong, Ivor?" laughed Jones. "Afraid of a bit of snow?"

They backed off and charged again.

Again, Ivor slammed on his brakes.

"Now, look here, Ivor," began Jones angrily
because he had bumped his nose. "Just what
do you . . ."

He stopped. He had seen something.

The snowpile was not all snow. Some of
it looked like wool.

Jones saw a nose here, an ear and a tail
there. He fetched his shovel.

"Baa," said the first sheep as he dug
it out.

Jones went on digging. He dug out in all,
fourteen sheep. They were very cold and
miserable, but they were unharmed.

"Baa-baa-baa-baa – Baa!" they shouted.

"Yes, all right," said Jones. "but do be
quiet a minute while we decide what to do
with you."

There was only one thing they could do
really; take the sheep to Llaniog and find
out to whom they belonged.

Jones unloaded all the goods, except
Miss Figgin's uncle. Then he lifted the
sheep into the trucks.

"They'll be company for you, Mr Figgin."

"Baa-baa-baa," said the sheep, very pleased.

"Bah!" said Mr Figgin, very displeased.

POOP-POOP! went Ivor's whistle.
CHUFF CHUFF CHUFF.

They charged through what remained of the snowheap and headed for home.

Everybody in Llaniog was out to meet them.

"Hooray for Jones, the hero!" they shouted. "Hooray for Ivor!"

"Have you brought my flour?" shouted Eli.
"My potatoes?" shouted Mr Davies.
"My bull's-eyes?" shouted Mrs Williams.
"Nothing but sheep!" shouted Eli angrily.
"Look! Two truckloads of sheep and if there
is one thing we have plenty of in Llaniog,
it is cold sheep!"

"Dashed impertinence!" muttered Mr Figgin.

"Where is my dolly-mixture?" wailed Mrs Williams.

POOOOOOOP went Ivor's whistle so loudly that everybody had to stop shouting.

"Now, listen everybody," said Jones
the Steam. "The goods are a mile or so
back down the line. We just unload the
sheep and go back for them . . . all right?"
They lifted down the sheep, and Mr Figgin
who was still bleating.

Jones and Ivor went back down the line, and Mr Davies and Eli the Baker came too because Jones the Steam had lifted enough boxes and bags for one day.

So the sheep came home, Mr Davies got his potatoes, Mrs Williams her bull's-eyes and the next day Eli the Baker made a batch of hot fresh rolls for them all.

This edition published 1994 by Diamond Books
77-85 Fulham Palace Road, Hammersmith London W6 8JB

First published by Picture Lions 1979
14 St James's Place, London SW1

© text and illustrations Oliver Postgate and Peter Firmin 1979

Printed in Slovenia

ISBN 0 261 66570-7